# THE HEARTLESS ROBOTS

A TEMPLAR BOOK

First published in 2010 by Templar Publishing,
an imprint of The Templar Company Limited,
The Granary, North Street,
Dorking, Surrey, RH4 1DN, UK
www.templarco.co.uk

1 3 5 7 9 10 8 6 4 2

ISBN 978-1-84877-031-7

Designed by Mike Jolley
Edited by Anne Finnis

Printed in the United Kingdom

BOB & BARRY'S LUNAR ADVENTURES

# THE HEARTLESS ROBOTS

# SIMON BARTRAM

templar publishing
www.templarco.co.uk

# IDENTITY CARD

Name: **Bob**

Occupation: **Man on the Moon**

Licence to Drive: **space rocket**

Planet of residence: **Earth**

Alien activity: **unaware**

**WORLDWIDE ASTRONAUTS' ASSOCIATION**

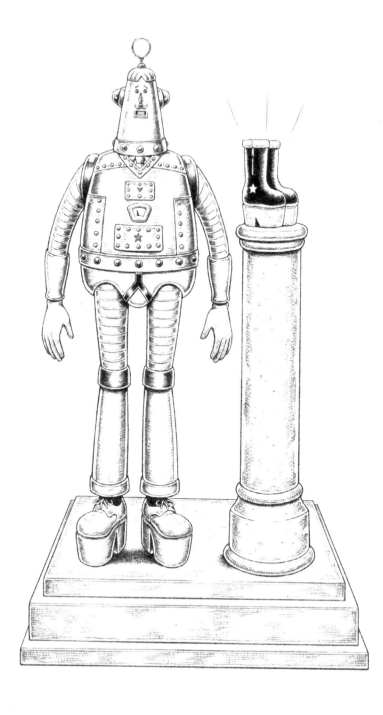

# CHAPTER ONE

The TV studio was mouse quiet. The tension was almost unbearable. The moment had come.

The final two astronauts in the *Spacemen Who Are Also Inventors' Inventions Competition* stood side by side, each desperately hoping to hear the host of the evening, Dermot Pilkington-Fizz, read out his name, declaring him the competition winner.

Bob, the Man on the Moon, accompanied by his unusual six-legged dog, Barry, had everything, including his eyes, firmly crossed. His invention, The Galaxobot 3000, was a triumph of brain-thinking. Bob had built the state-of-the-art robot

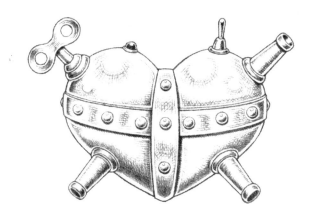

to be a super-servant for the overworked modern spaceman. It would be a caretaker, a butler, a chauffeur, a chef and more besides. Its motto was "HAPPY TO HELP". In fact, helping was all it was programmed to do. Deep inside its metal chest was its crowning glory, a breathtaking gold mechanical heart. Constructed from an orchestra of nuts, bolts, screws and cogs, the heart buzzed and ticked and tocked and clicked, sending waves of kindness to every nook and cranny of its mighty frame. The Galaxobot 3000 would be a blessing to all astronauts.

Only the other finalist, Stan the Man on Gas Mark 5, disagreed about that. His invention, a pair of Incredible Edible Spaceboots was also a work of genius. The stylish boots, made mainly of cake, were designed for cosmic hikers who were lost in space and low on sandwiches. A quick nibble here and there would keep their hunger at bay until a rescue rocket arrived. There was even a special hidden compartment in each platform sole in which dry-roasted peanuts and smallish pickled onions could be stashed. It was a simple but brilliant idea and, having been runner-up for the previous five years, Stan was convinced that it was his turn to win.

Dermot Pilkington-Fizz took a deep breath. "Ladies and gentlemen, boys and girls," he announced, "your votes have been counted and we have a result!" The audience went completely silent. "The winner of this year's *Spacemen Who Are Also Inventors' Inventions Competition* is…

BOB, THE MAN ON THE MOON, AND HIS
GALAXOBOT 3000!!!"

The studio erupted with noise and colour as confetti and streamers danced down from above. Bob was stunned. His now un-crossed eyes glazed over with happy tears that plip-plopped onto Barry who had excitedly leaped into his master's arms. Victory celebrations were new to Bob – his sideboard showed a definite lack of any kind of twinkly trophy or medal. For Bob, this was a dream come true.

The audience cheered as Dermot Pilkington-Fizz presented Bob with his grand prize. As well as a most terrific silver egg cup he was awarded two tickets for an amazing round-the-world super trip. Even better than that, though, was the promise that thousands of Galaxobots would be made. It was predicted that just about every astronaut in the universe would want one. Bob could not stop smiling.

   As the jubilant scenes continued, only one
sad soul stood motionless. Yet again, Stan the
Man on Gas Mark 5 had been pipped at the post
and was second best. His tears didn't glisten
under the spotlights. They were dark tears of red-
raw fury. This was one defeat too many. *Someone*
would have to pay.

But for now the night belonged to Bob. As he posed for photographs with his egg cup, all was right with the world. Or at least, that was what he thought. However, when the studio lights dimmed and the celebrations moved backstage, nobody noticed a shadowy figure lingering behind in the darkness. No one heard the clink-clanking as he tampered with Bob's Galaxobot 3000. And not a single pair of eyes witnessed the dastardly fiend slip away into the night, leaving behind a trail of cake-crumb footprints and a universe that was destined for BIG, BIG TROUBLE!

# CHAPTER TWO

Bob had only been a boy when his Galaxobot idea had first sprung to life in a series of drawings, doodles and diagrams. In no time at all, his bumper sketchbook had become a bulging super construction instruction manual. Following it carefully, he then began to build his dream. It was a mammoth task that would take years. At first, Bob's Grandad Bill had been around to help, occasionally making the odd addition to the manual. However, as Bob had grown older, he'd spent more and more spare time alone, tinkering and tweaking, until at long last his splendid Galaxobot was finished. Then, one fateful day, he'd seen the

Inventors' Inventions Competition advertised in *The Daily Bugle* and the rest was history.

Now that Bob had won the competition, the Galaxobot factory was quickly up and running. It was built on the Moon so that, as the inventor, Bob could be on hand to pass on top tips and brilliant advice. Whereas it had taken him years and years to construct his Galaxobot prototype, the state-of-the-art factory would be able to produce a truck load of them every single day. It was going to be amazing.

Lovingly, Bob named his Galaxobot prototype Mr Nigel Carruthers and, to identify him as the original, he carved a number one into his rear end. Surprisingly, Bob felt a pang of sadness on delivering him to the factory to be closely studied and copied. He was reassured, however, that Mr Nigel Carruthers would be returned to Earth in plenty of time to welcome Bob and Barry home from their round-the-world super trip.

And so, with a smile, they travelled the Earth and the Earth didn't disappoint. Bob buzzed with new experiences: he cycled on the 'wrong' side of the road; he dared to sample exotic delicacies such as garlic bread and chicken chop suey; and there was drama in a place called Pisa when Bob urgently informed the emergency services that the city's tower was leaning dangerously and about to fall over.

"Phew, Barry," he said, "it's a good job we were passing!"

Like all good trips, though, it had to come to an end. In truth, Bob was looking forward to having Mr Nigel Carruthers welcome them home with a nice cup of tea and a foot rub. Yet, on their return, he and Barry were completely horrified. In the garden, plants and flowers had been destroyed, gnome heads had been scattered everywhere, and cat drawings had been graffitied across poor Barry's kennel. Cautiously, they peeped through

Bob's living room window. Inside, the wool from countless unravelled tank tops was draped over toppled lamps and smashed ornaments. Precious football stickers had been slapped all over the walls, the ceiling and the floor. The carpet was thick with mouldy fish paste. And, to top it all, a felt-tip moustache had been scrawled onto Bob's signed portrait of his favourite cowboy film star, Clint 'Ten-Gallon' Hat. As if the house itself were terrified, it was shaking to its very foundations as heavy metal music blasted out from one of the TV music channels.

Just then, a cackling Mr Nigel Carruthers charged into the room with a pair of underpants on his head. He looked different. His eyes shone a wicked red and his gentle nature seemed to have disappeared altogether. With thrashing arms and legs he feverishly head-banged to the music until finally he lost his balance and crashed violently into the TV, causing it to explode.

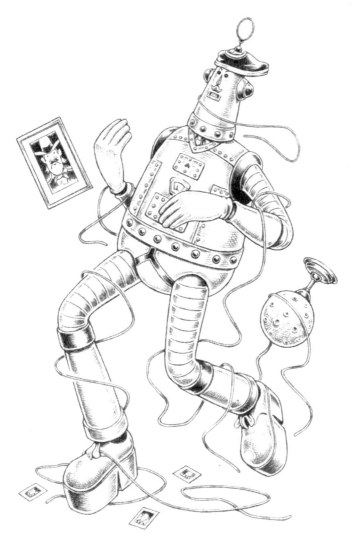

Bob and Barry were in a state of shock. As an eerie calm settled upon the smoky room, tears flooded Bob's eyes and he began to cry. This proved to be disastrous. With the TV blown up, there was now no music to drown out Bob's sobs.

Suddenly, through the haze, a pair of red eyes appeared at the window directly in front of them.

"HE'S GOING TO ATTACK!" screamed Bob. "RUN FOR YOUR LIFE, BARRY!!!"

And run they did – out of the town, through the woods, over the hills, all the way to the Lunar Hill launch pad.

"WE'VE GOT TO GET TO THE MOON QUICK-SHARP!" panted Bob. "WE'LL BE SAFE THERE!" Worryingly, at that moment, he noticed that his rocket was filthy and full of dents. As he frantically changed into his Man on the Moon suit, his inner voice begged him not to climb aboard, but he ignored it. Opening the hatch, he and Barry clambered into the cockpit only to make another shocking discovery. Sitting, bold as brass, in the pilot seat was a second mean-looking Galaxobot.

"Hello, Bob!" it said, menacingly. "WE'VE BEEN EXPECTING YOU!"

In a blind panic Bob and Barry circled around to make their escape. But blocking the hatch was Mr Nigel Carruthers himself! They were well and truly trapped.

Just minutes later, having been tightly tied up and roughly shoved into the mini-loo, they felt the rocket rumble and explode upwards through space. It wasn't long before they realised where they were being taken. Bob recognised each zoom, turn and swoop of his rocket. If his calculations were correct, in no time at all they would be landing ON THE MOON!

# CHAPTER THREE

The smelliest and most miserable rocket flight in history came to an end after just fifteen minutes and, sure enough, Bob and Barry were rudely pushed out onto the lunar surface.

It certainly was the Moon, but not as they knew it. It seemed darker and colder and, like their home, it was in a terrible state. Disturbingly, Galaxobots were patrolling everywhere and a most villainous streak seemed to be buzzing through their circuitry.

"LOOK!" cackled one of them. "IT'S BOB THE WASTE-OF-SPACEMAN!"

"AND HIS LUNAR-MUTT, LARRY!" bellowed another. A barrage of boos followed.

Bob was puzzled. "I'm almost sure they should be programmed to call me 'sir' or 'm'lord'," he muttered.

Immediately, however, his attention was needed elsewhere. Around him he was shocked to see that all of the craters had jail-like bars across their openings. Then, out of crater 198, a hand popped up and started waving frantically at Bob and Barry. A familiar voice swam through the sea of heckles. It belonged to Dick, the Man on Gigantorious B.

"ALL BUT TWO OF THE ASTRONAUTS IN THE UNIVERSE HAVE BEEN CAPTURED," he cried. "YOU AND STAN THE MAN ON GAS MARK 5 ARE THE ONLY ONES LEFT! RUN FOR YOUR LIFE!!!"

But it was too late. Bob was surrounded by Galaxobots and they looked tough. Unfortunately, he wasn't much of a boxer and he'd never been able to eat enough cake to grow into a decent-sized sumo wrestler. For now, at least, he would have to toe the line as he and Barry were forced down into crater 199 and locked in.

When the Galaxobots had trooped away, a confused Bob gazed at the stars through the bars. He daydreamed of flying amongst them once again and, for a fleeting moment, he felt happy. Then something bashed him on the helmet. It was a chunk of Moon rock with a piece of Gigantorious B notepaper wrapped around it.

"It's a letter from Dick!" whispered Bob to Barry. Skilfully, it had been tossed up from Dick's crater and down into their own.

Gigantorious 8

Dear Bob,

Universe in deep trouble! New Galaxobots gone proper bonkers! Took control of factory, THEN THE WHOLE MOON!! Destroying it with bullying and terrible vandalism. Are planning to take over rest of universe too! Massive Galaxobot army being built in factory.

Original workers exhausted and too slow. Galaxobots got very annoyed. Needed more workers. TRICKED ASTRONAUTS!! Lured us here with a message that our Galaxobots were ready to be picked up. We arrived. GOT CAPTURED! Now WE have to help build army too! Worse still, OUR PLANETS, MOONS AND ASTEROIDS ARE LEFT UNGUARDED AGAINST GALAXOBOT INVASION! Want to weep. Cosmos on brink of destruction.

Must go, don't want to get caught.

Dick xx

PS: How was the world trip? Isn't Rome lovely?

Bob could hardly take it all in. How could his wonderful invention have turned out to be so rotten? It didn't make any sense.

Just then, a piercing siren interrupted Bob's thoughts and the gate of his crater-jail was whipped open.

"OUT! NOW! TIME FOR WORK!!" ordered a grumpy Galaxobot as he poked and prodded Bob into a long line of marching astronauts. They were on their way to the factory.

With Barry in tow, Bob could now see for himself the shocking state of the place he loved the most. Whole Moon chunks were being destroyed during laser gun play-fights. Galaxobots were having fierce rally races, leaving crashed, burned out Moon buggies all over the place. Oil filled

craters, designed to be robot paddling pools, were overflowing, slowly turning the golden landscape black. And terribly rude pieces of graffiti were daubed everywhere like ugly tattoos.

Bob now realised what was in store for the rest of the universe. He felt sadder than he thought it was possible to be. This time though, his eyes shed no tears. They'd been distracted by a hazy blot on the horizon that began to take shape as they marched closer. It was the Galaxobot factory.

Bob was flabbergasted. It was enormous – ten times bigger than it had been when Bob dropped off Mr Nigel Carruthers. It heaved with dark chimneys and was caged in by vicious barbed wire. Above the entrance there was a chilling sign that read, '10 DAYS UNTIL INVASION'.

Inside, the din was deafening. Hot machinery clanked and clunked, pinged and chugged, spitting out a long line of troublesome Galaxobots onto an ever-moving conveyor belt. As the astronaut shift began, Bob wondered how exactly he'd managed to place the universe in such danger? Consigned to the moustache and wig department, he was sure of only one thing. It was up to him to put things right!

# CHAPTER FOUR

Work, eat, sleep. Work, eat, sleep. That was the pattern that soon took over Bob and Barry's lives. The hard labour was exhausting and the food was hardly fit to eat. Sleep became their only comfort. However, after much thinking and worrying, Bob decided that even their dreams would have to be put on hold. The few hours they were allowed for sleep would be needed for more important tasks. The sign on the factory now read, '5 DAYS UNTIL INVASION'. Next to it a huge poster had been put up advertising, 'THE GRAND GALAXOBOT INVASION CELEBRATION DISCO AND NUT BUFFET'.

The twenty-four hour party was to take place just before the Galaxobots invaded the entire universe. Time was running out.

"Listen, Barry," said Bob. "Until we know what's gone wrong with the Galaxobots, we can't put things right. We've got to have a good nose around that factory, to sniff out a clue or two. And we must get in there undetected."

Bob's super Moon knowledge was going to prove vital. Firstly, using moustaches 'borrowed' from their department as tools, they scraped and dug their way through their crater-jail floor until the last of it crumbled away and they tumbled

 downwards into a maze of underground tunnels. Bob had to be brave. He wasn't fond of the dark, but he tippy-toed his way through the mysterious twists and turns. As well as following

the Moon-map imprinted on
his brain, he swore he could
hear voices guiding him
and Barry onwards. And
soon, oddly, those voices
were accompanied by
riotous heavy metal music

that slowly became louder and louder. Gradually
the tunnels began to shake, rattle and roll until
Bob and Barry were almost in the epicentre of the
din. It was coming from above them.

"If I'm correct," deduced Bob, "we're directly
underneath the Galaxobot factory!"

Using their moustache tools, they scraped at
the tunnel above their heads. A crack of light
appeared. The crack then widened to become a
hole – a hole just big enough for a space dog and
an astronaut to scramble up through, which they
did. As their eyes adjusted to the light, they knew
that they were inside the Galaxobot factory, but

30

they didn't recognise the cavernous control room around them. Three of its walls flicked and clicked under a patchwork of dials, switches and monitors. The fourth was dominated by a huge map of the Universe on which every doomed planet, moon and asteroid was marked with an ominous red skull. Curiously, only the gleaming Gas Mark 5, which had a smiley face felt-tipped onto it, seemed destined for better times.

Below the map, the source of the now unbearably loud music was revealed. With its back to Bob and Barry, a Galaxobot DJ was furiously spinning tunes on a most impressive CD super-machine.

"TESTING 1-2! TESTING 1-2!!" it shouted into a microphone. "WELCOME TO THE GRAND GALAXOBOT INVASION CELEBRATION DISCO AND NUT BUFFET. IT'S TIME TO ROCK ON AND PARTY HAAAARRRDD!!!"

Using space sign-language to cut through the racket, Bob 'spoke' to Barry.

"The disco isn't for days. This must be a rehearsal," he reckoned, as they heard the Galaxobot repeat the same lines over and over, spinning CD after CD. Steadily, it whipped itself up into a frenzy before finally it opened up a hatch in its belly, took out a handful of darts and hurled them violently at the universe map.

"WE'RE COMING TO GET YOU!!!" it shouted mercilessly.

Bob was horrified. Barry was too, although his attention seemed to be elsewhere – straight above him to be exact. Bob followed his gaze and was astounded at what he saw. The ceiling was covered by a huge painting of Stan the Man on Gas Mark 5. He was sitting on a large, golden throne, eating a pair of Incredible Edible Spaceboots, as Galaxobots fanned his face and filed his toenails.

"CRUMBS ALIVE!" Bob cried, forgetting to use space sign-language. "WHAT'S STAN GOT TO DO WITH ALL OF THIS?"

They would not get the chance to find out. Disastrously, Bob had spoken during a minuscule gap between songs. At once, the Galaxobot swivelled around, its devilish gaze landing upon the intruders. Bob's life flashed before his eyes. The music began again with a tune that seemed far too jolly to be the soundtrack to their final moments.

"HE'S GOING TO ATTACK!" yelled Bob, falling to his knees. "THIS IS THE END, BARRY! GOODBYE, MY LOVELY FRIEND!"

However, after an excruciating wait, the end didn't come. A few seconds later, they dared to open their eyes. Strangely, although still towering above them menacingly, the Galaxobot had conked out cold. Bob and Barry were astonished. They couldn't believe their luck. Cautiously, with a mixture of terror and relief, Bob circled it and noticed a small number one, carved into its rear-end. It was his prototype – MR NIGEL CARRUTHERS!!! BINGO! It was time to investigate. What had poisoned that beautiful mechanical soul? Carefully, Bob opened the chest access-panel. The answer was obvious straight away. Not a solitary tick tocked. Not a single glimmer shimmered. The all-important heart of gold WAS GONE! Mysteriously, in its place sat an ordinary, bog-standard rock – a dark heart of stone. It was a disaster!

# CHAPTER FIVE

Even though someone else had obviously tampered with Mr Nigel Carruthers, Bob blamed himself for the way the Galaxobots had turned out. During the building of the prototype he had carried out umpteen tests to see how its fiddly robotic machinery would react with the beautiful golden heart. The results had always been good, never once though had it crossed his mind to test how the same robotic machinery would react WITHOUT the golden heart. Somehow, the absence of a golden heart turned any Galaxobot into a nasty piece of work and, as things stood, that was all of them. Each one had clearly been modelled on the evil Mr Nigel Carruthers. To save the universe, Bob realised he would have to create a golden heart for every Galaxobot and find a way to install each one. He had to give the robots the kindness he'd always intended them to have.

"I need my construction instruction manual," he decided. "I may be the supreme Galaxobot expert but it won't hurt to give it a swift once over, just to be on the safe side!"

Unfortunately, the manual was in his garden shed, at home. They had to get to Earth and pronto.

Bob and Barry set off through the cold factory corridors, desperately hoping not to bump into a grumpy Galaxobot. What they really needed was a clever disguise to help them blend into the surroundings.

And then, amazingly, they had a stroke of luck. They spotted a door with a sign that read: 'BITS AND BOBS AND BITS OF BODS.'

 Inside were shelves packed with Galaxobot components – heads, bodies, arms, legs, the lot.

"Just the ticket!" smiled Bob who then set about piecing together a new Galaxobot. But this was a Galaxobot with a difference. It was hollow! Or at least it was until Bob and Barry climbed inside. Fifteen minutes later, wearing it like a suit of armour, they calmly walked out of the factory, across the Moon and towards Bob's trusty rocket. None of the Galaxobots outside detected a thing.

"Off to round up some more snivelling humans?" asked one of them.

"AFFIRMATIVE!!" Bob fibbed convincingly.

Minutes later, back on Earth, Bob had to fight back the tears that welled in his eyes at the sight of his battered home. But there was no time to feel sorry for himself. After a banana sandwich and a quick trim of his nose hair, he popped out to the shed to save the universe.

Bob's construction instruction manual was a dog-eared jumble of Galaxobot information. It had been glued and glittered and airbrushed and painted and patched up and sneezed on. As Bob opened it he immediately remembered wet weekends and summer holidays, laughing and learning with his Grandad Bill.

He closely studied the Golden Heart section, then, over a comforting cuppa he decided to thumb through the rest of the manual. And that's when he noticed two tea-stained pages that had become stuck together. Carefully, Bob prised them apart and found that they were two pages of notes that his grandad must have put in.

"Wow, Barry!" said Bob. "I've never even seen these before."

Curiously, the left-hand page was a piece of battered sheet music titled 'The Robot Foxtrot Cha-Cha Song', whilst the right was a message for him from Grandad Bill.

Dear Bob,

While you were at the football sticker convention I thought I would program a special deactivation code song into your Galaxobot. Whenever it hears this particular song, it will conk out for exactly fifteen minutes. You never know when that might come in handy. The song I've chosen is my favourite in the hit parade, 'The Robot Foxtrot Cha-Cha Song'. (You can change it for something more hip if you want.)

Love, Grandad xx

"Blimey!" said Bob. "A song that makes the Galaxobots conk out for fifteen minutes? That's music to my ears! I must find out how it goes."

Excitedly, he rushed into the house and returned with his bagpipes and, following the sheet music, began to play. The notes that emerged formed a tune that Bob recognised at once. IT WAS THE SAME TUNE THAT HAD BEEN PLAYING

WHEN MR NIGEL CARRUTHERS HAD
CONKED OUT, MID-ATTACK!

"WOW!" cheered Bob. "IT WORKS!"

Bob couldn't believe his chunk of good
fortune. If 'The Robot Foxtrot Cha-Cha Song'
had not been played right then in that control
room, he and Barry would have been gonners!
And then it hit him.

"Wait a minute, Barry!" he beamed.
"If the song was played during the disco
rehearsal then it will be played during
the real thing! And, if it works
again, each and every Galaxobot
will conk out for fifteen minutes!
That will be our big chance to
install the new golden hearts!
BINGO!!"

# CHAPTER SIX

It was a pity Infinity House, the headquarters for the entire universe, was temporarily closed. As Bob walked past he could see painters and decorators inside. The staff were all on holiday. The Head of the Department for Moon Affairs, Tarantula Van Trumpet would probably have been able to solve all the trouble in an instant if he hadn't been off pot-holing somewhere or other.

Bob was on his way to use the photocopier at the library next door to Infinity House. It was essential that he made as many copies as possible of the 'Golden Heart' section of his manual. He would need them later. More importantly, though, he needed a huge stash of gold to make the new hearts from. This was a major problem. Gold didn't grow on trees and not once during his round-the-world super trip had he come across a town where the streets were paved with it.

Back at home Bob stood in the garden and stared at the Moon. Covered in dark, oil-slicky spots, it appeared tired and ill and ready to infect the cosmos around it.

"I think we need a miracle, Barry," said Bob.

Then, as if on cue, a speck of light pinged to life near crater 738. Soon after, another appeared and then another until a long curved line of lights gleamed as if the Moon were smiling. Bob had no choice but to blast upwards for a closer look.

Luckily, the sparkles had appeared on a part of the Moon that the Galaxobots had already ravaged and therefore abandoned. As Bob's rocket approached, the twinkles guided him in like the lights of an airport runway and, on landing, Bob's heart soared at what he saw. Each sparkle was a beautiful golden nugget, bright enough to shine through the darkest of times. Safely back in their Galaxobot disguise, Bob and Barry followed the nugget trail which led to a crater. Oddly, Bob didn't recognise it. Cautiously, they peeped inside and were flabbergasted. Before their eyes was a gold mine vast enough to make double the amount of golden hearts that could ever be needed and then

 some. Despite his confusion, Bob was ecstatic.

There were now only four days left until the Grand

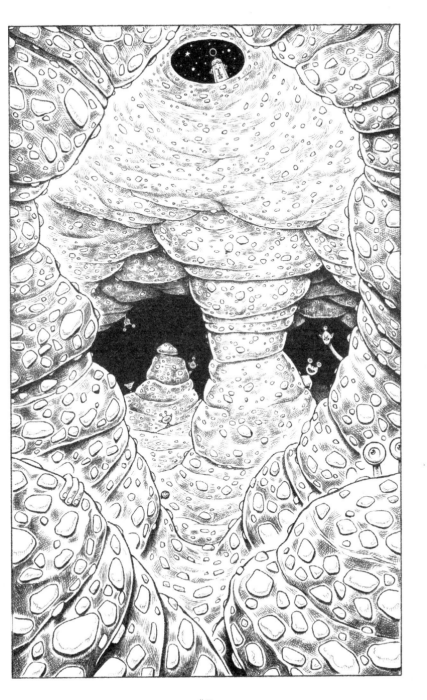

Galaxobot Invasion Celebration Disco and Nut Buffet and there was much work to do. Bob and Barry, using their faithful moustache tools, toiled tirelessly mining the gold. Time and again they filled the spare space inside their Galaxobot disguise with nuggets, before clunking their way to the crater-jails where they distributed the gold amongst the astronauts. The Galaxobots were too busy having their terrible fun to notice anything unusual. They never once twigged that Bob and Barry were missing. Neither did they notice the disappearance of hundreds of tools from the factory or the constant hammering and tapping that came from the crater-jails when the astronauts were supposed to be sleeping. Following Bob's photocopied construction instructions the spacemen worked endlessly to build up a stockpile of golden hearts. It was a race against time. Not only did they have to construct a heart for every existing Galaxobot but also for every Galaxobot yet to be made – production would not stop until the invasion began.

Two days before the disco, a huge dance floor was laid on the Moon's surface. It was lined with powerful loudspeakers to relay the music from the control room. A bar was installed offering  oily cocktails to accompany the nut buffet and rivet snacks. Bunting was hung and banners bearing the image of Stan the Man on Gas Mark 5 were unfurled.

Bob had been thinking about Stan a lot. Could HE have had anything to do with Mr Nigel Carruthers' unfortunate change of heart?

But Bob had to put Stan to the back of his mind for now.

Soon enough it was the evening before the big day and the last soldier of the Galaxobot army rolled off the conveyor belt. It was surrounded by its cheering comrades, including Bob and Barry, still in their disguise as Bob was keen to get a quick peek at the robot's rear end. The number carved into it would reveal the exact amount of Galaxobots in existence. He then snuck back to the crater-jails and passed on this information to the busy astronauts.

A little while later each astronaut revealed with a whisper the number of golden hearts he'd been able to make. Carefully, Bob added up the figures on his brain-abacus. Would the golden hearts match the number of Galaxobots? It all came down to Dirk the Man on Maximars. Twenty-two more hearts were needed. Nervously, Bob asked for his total.

"Twenty-one," he chirped, "plus of course, the one I'm finishing at the moment!"

"BINGO!" thought Bob.

For now they could do no more. The fate of the universe rested with 'The Robot Foxtrot Cha-Cha Song'. If it deactivated the Galaxobots at the disco then Bob's plan just might stand a chance. If not, all of their hard work would have been in vain.

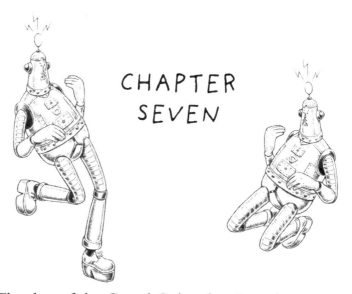

# CHAPTER SEVEN

The day of the Grand Galaxobot Invasion Celebration Disco and Nut Buffet arrived. In twenty-four hours, using the rockets they'd confiscated from the astronauts, the army of Galaxobots would be blasting off to cause havoc in every corner of the cosmos. First, though, they had some serious partying to do.

From deep inside the factory control room, Mr Nigel Carruthers launched into the first tune of the bash. Outside, the dance floor exploded into life, as rip-roaring heavy metal music blasted through the loudspeakers. The Galaxobots whipped themselves up into a frenzy, head-banging and strumming their air guitars. Bob and Barry, still in their disguise, had no choice but to join in. In truth, heavy metal music wasn't Bob's kind of thing. He much preferred the sweet sound of bagpipes or the occasional banjo tune. Soon he longed for a quiet sit down with a nice cup of tea and a puzzle book. However, saving the universe had to come first.

Nervously, Bob waited for 'The Robot Foxtrot Cha-Cha Song' to be played. Everything was prepared for that moment. Sneakily, he had unlocked every crater-jail and the astronauts were waiting inside, poised to jump out and fit the new hearts into the deactivated Galaxobots. But things weren't going to plan.

As cocktails were guzzled and the buffet was gobbled, the metal got heavier and the clock ticked on at a pace. In no time the party was half over. Soon enough only ten hours remained, then five, then three – then two and one. The crucial deactivation song had not been played. A seed of doubt began to grow in Bob's brain. Had 'The Robot Foxtrot Cha-Cha Song' *really* been playing when Mr Nigel Carruthers had conked out? Was it *really* on the disco play list? Closing his eyes tightly Bob tried to remember. To his great relief, he recalled that the vital deactivation song had indeed been playing, but, to his dismay, he recollected something awful that he must have pushed to the back of his mind. Below the CD super-machine there had been a cardboard box with the word REJECTIONS written on it. It was full to the brim with CDs. Suddenly, Bob understood. During rehearsal, whenever Mr Nigel

Carruthers didn't like a song, he'd simply tossed the CD into the rejections box! Thinking about it, 'The Robot Foxtrot Cha-Cha Song' didn't fit in at all with the raucous heavy metal that the Galaxobots loved. Mr Nigel Carruthers may have only heard two or three seconds of it before conking out but that would have been enough for him to realise that he hated it.

And then Bob knew. The song he desperately needed to deactivate the Galaxobots was deep inside that box, never to be played again. His plan lay in tatters, but Bob refused to give up.

"We *have* to find 'The Robot Foxtrot Cha-Cha Song' quick-sharp," he said, as he and Barry slipped quietly into the factory and out of their cumbersome disguise. Having found their way

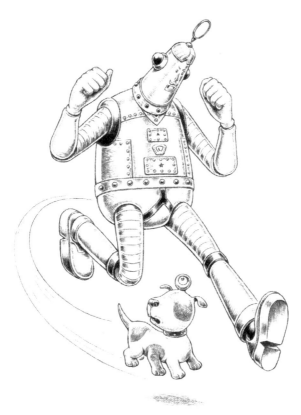

back through the maze of corridors they were soon, once again, peeking through the control room door. Mr Nigel Carruthers was dancing wildly by the CD super-machine. Bob looked at Barry and, with space sign-language, asked him to do a most important job. Barry woofed the bravest of woofs. And so, as Bob hid, his faithful friend sprinted into the room boldly distracting the outraged Galaxobot. Then Barry quickly pulled a sharp U-turn and dashed back out again with Mr Nigel Carruthers hot on his tail. Bob was free to rummage through the rejections box in search of the all-important CD. Unfortunately, it was nowhere to be seen. Bob felt beaten. Things couldn't get any worse.

Until, of course, they did, when a cold voice emerged from a darkened corner of the room. "Is *this* what you're looking for?"

Bob recognised the voice long before Stan the Man on Gas Mark 5 stepped out of the shadows. In one hand he was holding 'The Robot Foxtrot Cha-Cha Song' CD and in the other he was holding a ray gun.

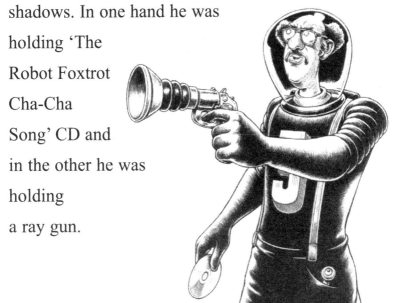

# CHAPTER EIGHT

If he'd had to hazard a guess, Bob would have said that Stan the Man on Gas Mark 5 was a little bit miffed about something.

"So, Bob," spat the competition runner-up, "here we are, together again. Just in time for the downfall of the universe which, in people's eyes, will be ALL YOUR FAULT!!!"

Bob looked shocked.

"Oh, yes," continued Stan. "It was I who installed the first heart of stone and it was I who nurtured the wickedness within it. And indeed, I've masterminded the glorious Galaxobot invasion from afar. But it is YOU the people will blame.

It was *your* Galaxobot they cast their vote for, and *your* Galaxobots they shall run from in fear. They know nothing of my meddling. It will be *your* head they shall demand. And then that glorious first prize will be stripped from you and awarded to ME. And my Incredible Edible Spaceboots will become famous! The demand will be huge. A million pairs are ready and waiting on Gas Mark 5. As the Galaxobots were multiplying, I was baking furiously. Now, I am ready to take my place in history – a ruined universe is a small price to pay!"

Then Stan teasingly held aloft the deactivation CD. Bob's eyes widened.

"You really want this, don't you, Bob?" said Stan. "I saw you, on monitor 27, entering the factory.

I lip-read your words. I know how powerful you think this is. WELL, YOU'RE NOT GETTING IT! NO WAY, NO HOW!!!"

He tossed the CD up into the air and aimed his ray gun at it. In a split second 'The Robot Foxtrot Cha-Cha Song' would be blasted to smithereens. But, before he could pull the trigger, Stan began to sway on his feet as, from below, munching sounds could be heard. Both Bob and Stan looked down and saw Barry. He'd given

Mr Nigel Carruthers the slip and had been quietly nibbling away at the platform soles of Stan's Incredible Edible Spaceboots. The once-sturdy soles had now taken on the slender shape of an apple core. As if tottering on tiny stilts Stan wavered and wobbled before falling flat on his astonished face, dropping his ray gun. Skilfully with one hand, Bob picked it up and with the other caught the tumbling deactivation CD.

Now only minutes remained until the Galaxobot invasion was due to begin. After tying up Stan, Bob rushed over to the CD super-machine and immediately brought the heavy metal racket to an end. On the countless monitors, enraged Galaxobots could be seen shaking their fists and beating their chests. They were ready to riot. Unruffled, Bob inserted the deactivation CD and reached out to press PLAY. However, as the tip of his finger hovered over the button, he was roughly grabbed from behind. Mr

Nigel Carruthers had returned and he seemed more than a little bit angry. He began to crush Bob with an almighty bear hug. Bob could hardly breathe.

"It's up to you, Barry!" he croaked. "Do it! Do it! Do it now!!!"

And do it Barry did. Leaping onto the CD super-machine he stuck out his wonderful snout and pressed the big red button with PLAY written on it, releasing the pleasant opening chimes of 'The Robot Foxtrot Cha-Cha Song'. It was now or never. Two or three unbearable seconds passed as the Galaxobot's vice-like grip tightened further. For a second time Bob's life flashed before him and things looked grim. But then, for a second time, Mr Nigel Carruthers couldn't finish his

attack. To Bob's relief, the mad, red light in the Galaxobot's furious eyes was extinguished and his deathly grip loosened. Bob fell to the

floor. 'The Robot Foxtrot Cha-Cha Song' had worked like a dream. Mr Nigel Carruthers was totally deactivated!

Bob's attention immediately turned to the monitors on the wall on which he could see the disco area outside. One by one, the Galaxobots were grinding to a halt and, after just a few seconds, there wasn't the tiniest flicker of movement anywhere within the whole vast army. It was a wonderful sight but there was no time for celebration. The Galaxobots would be motionless for just fifteen minutes and each one needed a new golden heart.

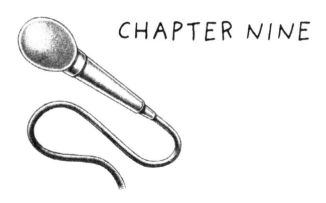

# CHAPTER NINE

The race was on. Bob decided to coordinate the whole delicate operation from inside the control room. He could see everything on the monitors and use the DJ microphone to address the astronauts outside.

"ALL CLEAR! ALL CLEAR!" he shouted. "CODE GREEN! GO, GO, GO!!!"

The astronauts sprang up and out of their unlocked crater-jails like jack-in-the-boxes, then sprinted to the disco floor, each carrying their own stash of golden hearts.

There was one heart for each Galaxobot. There were no spares. No second chances. Every heart had to work perfectly.

Step by step, closely following his construction instruction manual, Bob guided the astronauts through their crucial work. First, the chest access panels were prised open and the pesky hearts of stone were removed, to be replaced with the gleaming hearts of gold. Next followed the tricky task of knitting the hearts' fragile tubes into the complicated workings of the Galaxobots' chests. It was through these tubes that all the goodness would travel to the rest of the body. Bob could only pray that the double-sided sticky tape borrowed from the factory would be strong enough to hold them in place. He

also prayed that there was enough of it – there were so many hearts to fit. When the chest access panel of one completed Galaxobot was slammed shut, another was immediately opened.

All of the time Bob watched and directed the astronauts when they needed help. Some found the going easier than others. Mick, the Man on Minusculous 2, for example, worked so fast that his busy hands appeared blurry. However, Ron, the Man on Noo Yoik Noo Yoik, struggled as his sausage fingers were too chunky to cope with the fiddly wires and tiny screws. Many astronauts shook with nerves and some sweated so much

that their helmets began to steam up terribly.
Fortunately, when one astronaut began to flag,
another would jump in to help until finally, with
two minutes to spare, all of the golden hearts had
been fitted – all, that is, except for one which lay
twinkling in the moon dust. Bob and Barry stared
at it on monitor 17. The astronauts stared at it too.
Every last Galaxobot on the disco floor had been
fitted with a new heart. How could there be one
left over? Bob looked at Barry, Barry looked at
Bob, and then they both looked at Mr Nigel

Carruthers. Unbelievably, they'd forgotten to change *his* heart – the most important heart of all!

"HOLY HELMETS!" screamed Bob. "IN LESS THAN TWO MINUTES HE'S GOING TO REACTIVATE. HE'LL DESTROY US!!!"

They knew what they had to do. While Barry shot outside to collect the golden heart, Bob opened the chest access panel and discarded the dark heart of stone. Less than one minute remained to reactivation when Barry shot back into the control room with the heart in his mouth. Bob wasted no time. Roughly, he deposited the

heart, taped the tubes, screwed some screws and tweaked some wires and when the access panel was finally snapped shut there were just five seconds to spare.

Bob and Barry were close to collapse as they watched the clock count down 5 – 4 – 3 – 2 – 1! Silence. All of a sudden, a robotic finger wiggled on monitor 23. And then, on monitor 31, the faint twitch of a leg could be spotted. The Galaxobots were coming back to life. Nervously, Bob and Barry turned to Mr Nigel Carruthers just as he was beginning to stir. Very slowly, his back straightened and his limbs stretched. The moment of truth had arrived. WAS HE A FRIEND OR WAS HE A FOE?!

# CHAPTER TEN

With new life fizzing round his body, Mr Nigel Carruthers seemed taller and wider and stronger than before. This time though, Bob stared bravely straight into the eyes of the monster made by Stan's evil deed. Something was different. The wild fury had been replaced by a mesmerising sky-blue glow that began to hypnotise Bob. Vigorously, he shook his head and, refusing to be sucked into a false sense of security, he snapped out of his trance. Mr Nigel Carruthers slowly moved towards him and Bob took a step back.

"Get away!" shouted Bob. "I've got a ray gun! I don't want to use it but I will!"

Still the Galaxobot advanced until Bob had backed himself into a corner. He had nowhere to go. It seemed as if the golden hearts had failed.

Then, slowly, Mr Nigel Carruthers opened up the hatch in his belly and reached in to pull something out. Bob panicked. Which gruesome

instrument of destruction was he about to face? A bow and arrow? A cat-o-nine-tails? A STINK BOMB? He had no choice but to aim his ray gun directly at Mr Nigel Carruthers.

"I'm sorry!" he cried, tightly closing his eyes. "It wasn't meant to be this way!"

Bob braced himself for the deafening zap he was about to fire, but suddenly the ray gun was snatched from his hand. Fully expecting that Mr Nigel Carruthers had wrestled it from him, Bob opened his eyes in dread, only to see a beaming Barry with the gun clenched between his teeth.

Mr Nigel Carruthers was clutching something entirely different and calmly offered it to Bob.

"Could I interest you in this nice cup of tea?" he asked. "And perhaps a tasty coconut ring to go with it?"

Bob was staggered. Gratefully, he took the tea and it was perfect. Semi-skimmed milk, no sugar, piping hot!

"Happy to help, m'lord," said Mr Nigel
Carruthers, bowing.

As Bob sipped the tea, he looked once again
into the Galaxobot's eyes. This time he felt
comforted. They were brimming with kindness.
With his strong, beating heart of gold, Mr Nigel
Carruthers was once again the robot Bob had
intended him to be. Bob almost cried.

Outside, there wasn't a hint of trouble
anywhere. In fact, the Galaxobots were being
incredibly helpful. One was providing the
astronauts with much-needed foot-rubs whilst
another was washing their helmets with soapy
water and a chamois leather.
The oil slicks were being
scrubbed away and the broken
Moon chunks were being
pieced back together with
superglue. The astronauts'
rockets that had been

confiscated by the Galaxobots were being repaired and polished and all the rude graffiti was removed with a good old helping of elbow grease.

It was decided that the factory should be closed immediately. There were more than enough Galaxobot 3000s in existence. When they finally zoomed away, each astronaut took three of them. In addition, every astronaut was given his own mini pork pie with the word 'Sorry' written in the pastry, and a copy of 'The Robot Foxtrot Cha-Cha Song', should they ever

encounter any future Galaxobot mischief. As things stood, though, the new hearts seemed to have worked perfectly. Every one of Bob's Galaxobots was now as good as gold. The universe had been saved!

As for Stan, he was sentenced by Tarantula Van Trumpet, the Head of the Department for Moon Affairs, to work unpaid for a whole week (except Wednesday) in Vera Crumble's bakery back on Earth. There he learned the valuable lesson that, though cakes needed to be edible, they didn't necessarily need to be incredible. Ordinary cakes for ordinary occasions were just as vital.

And Bob learned that, if he were to invent anything again, he must ensure that it wouldn't be likely to try and conquer the universe. Astronauts were always calling out for new and advanced kinds of toast racks and tea towels. Perhaps he would try something like that.

Bob also decided that his newly cleaned and restored home was probably not big enough to need Mr Nigel Carruthers to take care of it. Mr Nigel Carruthers agreed, and went on to live peacefully in the hills, serving the world by writing poetry about butter and the sun.

Meanwhile, Bob was delighted to be back at work on his mended Moon. There were no celebration parties or grand reopenings. When everything was cleaned up, Bob just quietly went about his lunar business, safe in the knowledge that all around him the universe was at peace.

# IT SAVED THE UNIVERSE!

## BUY IT NOW!

AVAILABLE IN ALL LEADING RECORD SHOPS
ACROSS THE GALAXY OR FREE WITH ANY
VACUUM CLEANER PURCHASED FROM

## WALTER FIGLEAF'S
BRILLIANT VACUUM EMPORIUM

THE ROBOT FOXTROT CHA-CHA SONG

SPECIAL RE-RELEASE

by THE ODDBALL TRIO

THE END